BALLET CAT

Dance! Dance! Underpants!

For Steph,
who may or may not have written the
funniest joke in the whole story

Text and illustrations copyright © 2016 by Bob Shea

All rights reserved. Published by Disney • Hyperion, an imprint of Disney Book Group.
No part of this book may be reproduced or transmitted in any form or by any means,
electronic or mechanical, including photocopying, recording, or by any information
storage and retrieval system, without written permission from the publisher.

For information address Disney • Hyperion,

125 West End Avenue, New York, New York 10023.

Printed in Singapore

Reinforced binding

First Edition, February 2016

10 9 8 7 6 5 4 3 2 1

FAC-019817-15288

Library of Congress Cataloging-in-Publication Data

Shea, Bob, author, illustrator.
Ballet Cat : Dance! dance! underpants! / by Bob Shea.—First edition.
pages cm

Summary: Ballet Cat and her friend Butter Bear have practiced a dance to
perform for an audience, but Butter Bear will need a lot of encouragement
to try the super-high leaps.

ISBN 978-1-4847-1379-2

[1. Ballet dancing—Fiction. 2. Encouragement—Fiction. 3. Bears—Fiction.
4. Cats—Fiction.] I. Title. II. Title: Dance! dance! underpants!

PZ7.S53743Bae 2016

[E]—dc23   2014049276

www.DisneyBooks.com

BALLET CAT

Dance! Dance! Underpants!

Bob Shea

DISNEP • HYPERION

LOS ANGELES   NEW YORK

Nice toe pointing, Butter Bear.
Now let's do some super-high leaps.
No, thank you, Ballet Cat.

Look at that fancy light. A leaping bear could hurt her head on a fancy light like that.

Dangerous?

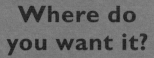

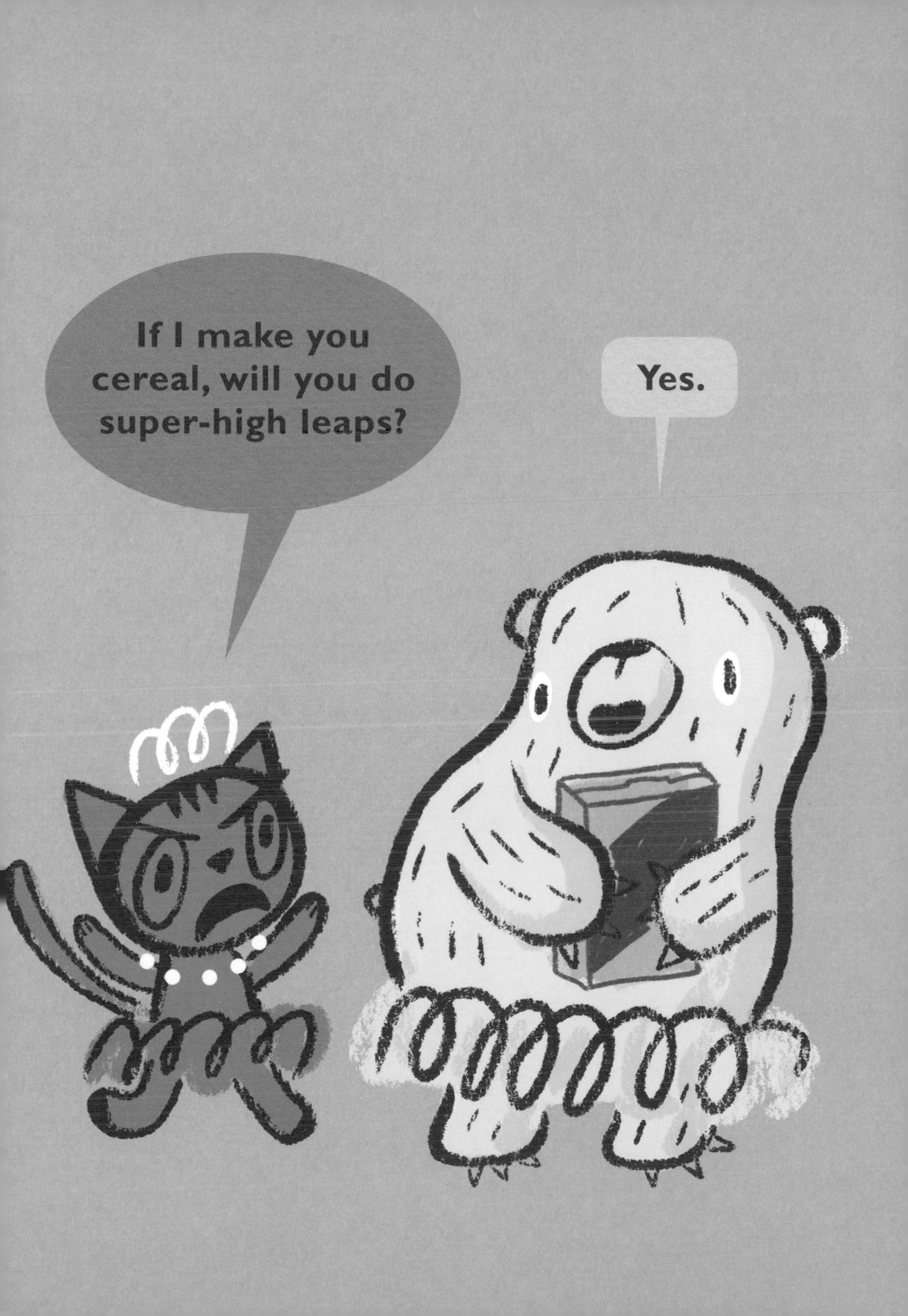
If I make you cereal, will you do super-high leaps?
Yes.

Oh, my goodness, you are right! It is very late.

No wonder I am so tired. I must go to sleep for the winter.

See you in the spring, Ballet Cat.

Not so fast!
You are not going anywhere until we do the super-high leaps like I showed you.
I cannot.

Come here. I have to
whisper it to you.

Whisper.
Whisper.
Whisper.

**If you dance with
all your heart, the only
thing they will see is the
beauty of ballet.**

**They will forget all about
your underpants.**